A Story from West Africa

Madoulina

A Girl Who Wanted to Go to School

by Joël Eboueme Bognomo

Boyds Mills Press

Published by Caroline House
Boyds Mills Press, Inc.
A Highlights Company
815 Church Street
Honesdale, Pennsylvania 18431
Printed in China

Publisher Cataloging-in-Publication Data
Bognomo, Joël Eboueme.
Madoulina / by Joël Eboueme Bognomo.—1st American ed.
[32]p. : col. ill. ; cm.
Originally published : Yaoundé, Cameroon :
Editions AKOMA MBA, 1996.
Summary : When her mother needs her to work all day in the
marketplace, a girl finds a way of continuing her education.
ISBN 1-56397-769-9 (hc.)
ISBN 1-56397-822-9 (pbk.)
1. Cameroon—Social life and customs—Juvenile fiction.
2. Mothers and daughters—Fiction—Juvenile literature. I. Title.
[E]—dc21 1999 AC CIP
Library of Congress Catalog Card Number 99-61826

First edition, 1999
Book cover designed by Randall Llewellyn
The text of this book is set in Sabon.

(hc.) 10 9 8 7 6 5 4 3 2
(pbk.) 10 9 8 7 6 5 4 3 2 1

This story is based on a play I wrote for television called *The Rebellion of Mpecka Madouline*, which was inspired by my conversations with Mrs. Sylvie Dickson Traore and Mrs. Marie Guerda Previllon of UNICEF. The play was my contribution to the African Light Theatre for the Day of the African Child.

Dedicated affectionately to all young African women,
and to my little sisters:
Estelle Dorette Ongouloli
Christelle Flore Kanena
Marguérite Francine Adoloma
Lydie Hortense Omboudombo
Gabrielle Egoli
and to my son, Rick Vannel Njoh Eboueme

My thanks to Marie Wabbes.

Let me tell you the story of how I was once like a bird who leaves the nest very early and only comes back late in the evening. I am Madoulina. Babo, my younger brother, and I lived with our mother in a small house in the Mokolo neighborhood in Yaoundé, Cameroon. My mother was poor but brave. Every day she went to the market to sell fresh produce and fritters.

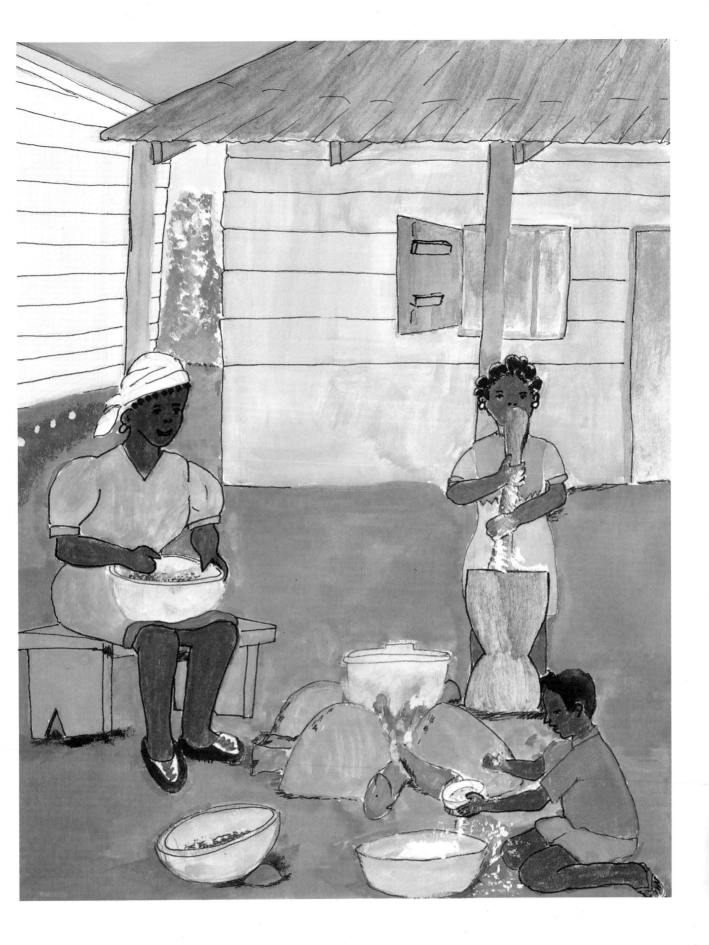

I had to help Mother. Every morning Babo went to school, but Mother kept me home.

Every day at six o'clock, Mother woke me up.

"Get up, Madoulina, it's time to sell fritters," she would say.

Sometimes I wished I could sleep longer, but I didn't want to disobey. So I would get up. Then, with a tray of fritters on my head, I went out into the street. Walking all around town selling fritters was not easy for someone my age.

One evening as school was letting out, one of the students started to tease me.

"Look, Babo's big sister is already selling fritters, just like her mom. Doesn't she want to be a doctor anymore?"

We started to argue.

All of a sudden a man came up to me and asked for some fritters. I wrapped a few for him.

"What's your name, little girl?" the man asked.

"My name is Madoulina," I replied.

"How old are you?"

"Eight."

"Ah! My name is Mr. Garba. I'm the new teacher."

"So you are my little brother Babo's teacher?" I asked.

"Yes, I am. But I've never seen you at school. Why?"

"Uh . . . well . . . I was supposed to start the first year of regular school, but my mother is poor. My father abandoned us, and my mother is raising us all alone. She would rather Babo went to school. As for me, I'm a girl, and when I grow up I'll get married. I'll take care of my husband and children."

"That may be, but school is very important also. Girls as well as boys must be educated. Meet me here tomorrow after school and take me to your house. I would like to speak to your mother."

So the next day I waited for Mr. Garba. It was getting dark when he arrived.

We walked in the moonlight, not speaking, along a little soccer field that led to the street where I lived. Piles of garbage lay here and there where hungry dogs came to feed. Most of the houses were old. Some, built out of planks, fit right in with the garbage cans. It was the poor part of town. People called it "Mokolo-Elobi"— the swampy area.

"Well, now!" said Mr. Garba. "This must be a real mosquito stronghold."

"Yes, sir, but we're used to their music. Here we are. This is where I live."

We went in. Mother was surprised to see me back late and not alone. She asked me who our guest was.

"It's Babo's teacher. Sir, this is my mother."

After the introductions, I gave Mother the day's earnings. Then I went to give my little brother a bath.

Mr. Garba tried to persuade Mother to send me to school. The two of them didn't seem to be getting along. Quickly, I finished giving Babo his bath, and we went back to the sitting room.

Mother was furious. She stood up.

"My dear sir," she said, "your arguments do not interest me at all. A woman is meant to look after a household."

"That's fine, ma'am," he said to her. "But if Madoulina went to school, she could look after a household even better. Besides, it's the right of all children to have an education — girls and boys."

These words went straight to my heart. They made me happy, even if they did not conquer the shadows in my heart.

"It's not her fault," I thought. My mother had never been to school. She just needed to understand what an education was.

"Times have changed," I said boldly to my mother. "Mr. Garba is right. I want to go to school, just like other children my age. I would like to be useful and take care of you, for example, when you are ill."

Mother was becoming more and more troubled. "Who will help me sell fritters if Madoulina no longer has time to help me?"

"I have an idea," said Mr. Garba. "If the fritters are the only problem, I can have a contract signed by the principal of the school. The school will buy the fritters Madoulina would have sold, and give them to our students. They will go well with the sandwiches that the students have during breaks."

This idea appealed to my mother. She accepted Mr. Garba's offer.

What joy! I was going back to school. Once more I could play with all my friends, and best of all, my dream of becoming a doctor could come true. It was the start of a new life! I thought about it all night.

In the morning, Mother took Babo and me to school. Mr. Garba gave me a book bag full of notebooks. After missing three weeks, I had to get caught up. There were many lessons to copy and learn. The day was hard, and I got home at night completely worn out.

Mr. Garba would not give up on us. He checked in on us every evening at home. He was very kind and friendly. At the end of every week he paid Mother's fritter bills. He became like a father to us.

At school I caught up with the rest of the class. I even helped my classmates with their homework when they ran into problems.

At the end of the term, Babo and I passed! Mother invited Mr. Garba to come celebrate with us. From then on we were a happy little family.